DATE DUE

Robyn Looks for Bears

Hazel Hutchins

Robyn Looks for Bears

Illustrations by Yvonne Cathcart

FIRST NOVELS

The New Series

Formac Publishing Company Limited
Halifax, Nova Scotia

Formac Publishing Company Limited acknowledges the support of the Cultural Affairs Section, Nova Scotia Department of Tourism and Culture. We acknowledge the financial support of the Government of Canada through the Book Publishing Industry Development Program (BPIDP) for our publishing activities. We acknowledge the support of the Canada Council for the Arts for our publishing program.

Canadian Cataloguing in Publication Data

Hutchins, H. J. (Hazel J.)
Robyn looks for bears

(First novels. The new series)

ISBN 0-88780-496-9 (pbk)
ISBN 0-88780-497-7 (bound)

I. Cathcart, Yvonne. II. Title. III. Series.

PS8565.U826R618   2000   jC813'.54   C99-950276-X
PZ7.H96162Ro 2000

Formac Publishing
Company Limited
5502 Atlantic Street
Halifax, NS B3H 1G4

Distributed in the U.S. by
Orca Book Publishers
P.O. Box 468 Custer, WA
U.S.A. 98240-0468

Printed and bound in Canada

Table of Contents

1
Thinking big

"This summer, I'm going to see a bear."

The Kelly twins sat in their buggy and looked up at me with their big, round eyes. They were only four months old. They didn't have any idea what I was talking about.

That was OK. I didn't really want anyone to know I was going to go looking for bears. Bears are big. And scary. And dangerous. But if you see one, you end up with a great story you can tell everyone for years and years.

I knew all about it. Every summer I'd heard bear stories at my aunt and uncle's cabins at Thunder Mountain. Every year, I'd wanted a bear story of my own to tell.

"I'll take a picture of the bear and send it to you," I told the twins.

We'd been for a walk around the block. Now I was taking them back to their mom, at the apartment right next door to mine. I think they knew I was leaving for a while. They gave me an extra wide smile as I said goodbye.

"Are you sure you'll be OK, Robyn?" my own mom asked for the tenth time on the way to the bus station the next morning.

Mom usually comes with me to Thunder Mountain. This year I was going alone.

"I'll be great," I answered. "You know how much I like Aunt Ellie and Uncle Paul. And Tim is super, even if he is older than me."

I sat right behind the bus driver. It was a three-hour trip to the mountains. I thought of all the great things the kids from school were doing for the summer. My best friend Marie was going to the ocean. Grant Smith, also known as Number One Twerp, was going to Disneyland. Some of the other kids were going to camp or across the country to see their grandparents.

All those things cost more money than my mom and I could afford, but I still felt really lucky. I was going to Thunder Mountain, and this year, I was going to have a bear story to tell.

2
Thunder Mountain

"You've come just in time!" cried Aunt Ellie.

She gave me a big hug as I stepped off the bus. Aunt Ellie loves to exaggerate.

"We're saved!" she cried.

There are twelve cabins, one main lodge, a million pine trees and a dog named Squirrel at Thunder Mountain. There's the mountain, too, of course. It's tall and beautiful, with great rocky cliffs. People on vacation love to take pictures of it. There were lots of people today. Lots and lots.

It really didn't take long for Aunt Ellie to put me to work. It's not hard work. I pick up the garbage around the cabins once a day. I help out at the main lodge. Aunt Ellie pays me when I leave. In between, I get paid in pop and ice cream.

Ten minutes later, I was cleaning car windows while my cousin Tim was pumping gas.

"We've got bubble-gum ice cream this year," he called from the back of the car he was filling.

"Is the pond deep enough for rafting?" I asked.

"Just right," said Tim.

"Did the tree fort survive the winter?" I asked.

"All except the roof," he said.

"Have you seen any bears around?" I asked.

"Nothing to worry about. Just a little black bear down by the laundry," said Tim.

Hurrah!

3
Now's my chance

It was huge and black and had little beady eyes and long sharp claws, but I wasn't afraid.

That night, lying in bed, I practised what I would tell my friends at school about the bear I was going to see.

"Are you talking in your sleep, Robyn?"

My bedroom is next to Tim's room, way at the top of the main lodge. The walls are very thin. Tim could hear me whispering to myself, even though he couldn't tell exactly what I was saying.

"No," I said. "I'm still awake."

"Do you want to look at the stars?" he asked.

The hall window opens right onto a small, flat piece of roof. On warm nights, Tim and I climb outside. It's safe, but it's really high up. It takes me a day or two to work up to being brave enough to go out there.

"Not tonight," I said. "Tell me about the tree fort."

That's what we talked about. We didn't talk about bears. I wasn't sure how Tim would feel about me wanting to see one.

But when I fell asleep, it was bears I dreamed about. Zoo bears, toy bears, bears on TV shows. Those were the only kind I'd ever seen. I'd never seen a wild one.

The next morning I woke up early. Early is a good time for seeing bears.

I dressed and found my camera. I went down to the kitchen. Anna, the lady who does the laundry, was having coffee with Aunt Ellie. The timing was perfect.

I snuck out the back door. Squirrel was lying on the back steps. He's a smart dog. He seemed to know we were looking for something.

We went quietly through the trees. Quietly past the

cabins. Quietly down towards the laundry building. Anna had already hung up a wall of sheets on the clothesline, so maybe it wasn't as early as I thought it was.

Suddenly, Squirrel stopped in his tracks and perked up his ears. Something was moving behind the sheets.

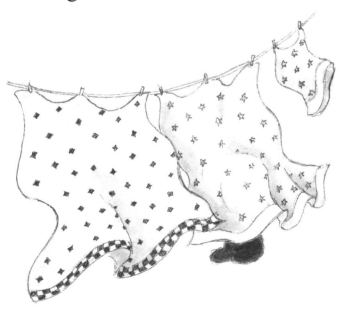

Something that made them
billow. Something that made
them bulge. It was big.
Beneath one sheet I could see
a big, black foot.
Bear!

4
Oh no!

"Bear!"

I didn't mean to shout. It just kind of burst out.

"Bear!"

Suddenly I was running up the path back to the main lodge.

"Bear! Bear! Bear!"

People came rushing out of the cabins. Aunt Ellie came running down from the lodge. Someone else came running too. That person was running mad and fast and was carrying a broom. It was Anna. I'd forgotten how mad Anna gets if anything dirties

her sheets when she hangs
them out to dry.

Like a crazy thing she raced
into the hanging sheets.

Wham! Whack!

The broom hit and hit and
Anna shouted.

"Out! Out of there!"

Wham! Whack!

I got my camera ready. Something came out of the sheets. It was wearing big black boots and holding its arms up to protect itself from the blows. It wasn't a bear. It was Uncle Paul!

Uncle Paul! Oh no!

"Wait, Anna! Wait!" I raced into the sheets to stop her.

When it was all over, Uncle Paul wasn't hurt. He began to explain about fixing the pully on the clothesline when something started hitting him. Pretty soon, he was laughing about it. Anna was laughing too. By lunch everyone was laughing and telling bear stories.

Everyone but me. I felt awful. That wasn't the kind

of bear story I'd wanted —
one without a bear. And why
had I run away shouting?
Was I some kind of scaredy
cat? Aunt Ellie seemed to
think so. The only good part
was that she didn't say so in
front of everyone else. She
took me quietly aside.

"From now on, Robyn,"
she said, "wait until later in
the day before you collect the
garbage. And make noise. That
way you won't have to worry
about bears."

And that way my chances
of going home with a bear
story, a real bear story, were
just about zero.

5
Mr. Sims

When things don't go the
way you want them to,
sometimes it makes you mad.
I tried not to be mad. I tried
to do other things instead.
But I couldn't forget about
bears. I'd promised the twins!
I'd promised myself!

A postcard arrived from my
friend Marie.

"Having a wonderful time,"
she wrote. "Wish you were
here." Marie isn't the best
person in the world at writing
postcards. On the bottom she

had added "Have you seen any bears yet?"

I'd forgotten about telling Marie I was going to see a bear this year. Probably I'd told her I was going to see one hundred or so. Probably I'd told Grant, the same thing. I get carried away sometimes.

As I sat in the lodge reading my card, Mr. Sims sat down beside me. Mr. Sims comes to the cabins every year to go fishing. I like him. He makes word games with my name.

"Now I know it's really summer," he said, "the robins are back."

I was just one Robyn, but I knew what he meant.

"Any luck this morning?" I asked.

"I didn't catch anything in the river," said Mr. Sims. "Tomorrow I'm going to hike up to Bear Lake."

Bear Lake! The name leapt out of the air as if it had gold and diamonds on it. With a name like that, there had to be bears!

"Would you take me with you?" I asked. "Could we be back by two o'clock?"

Two o'clock is the latest I can do my garbage pickup.

"We could," said Mr. Sims. His eyes twinkled. "That is, if you don't mind getting up with the robins."

6
I need wings

How early do the robins get up? 5:30 a.m.! The robins and the Robyns. And Tim, because we asked him to come too.

"It's almost seven kilometres each way, Robyn. Are you sure you still want to go?" Aunt Ellie asked as she handed me a bag lunch for my pack.

I nodded. How far could seven kilometres be?

The answer to that is — a long way. A long, long, long way. All of it uphill. Up and up and up.

At first I ran ahead. And then I ran and rested. And then I walked along beside Mr. Sims and Tim thinking thoughts like, why don't they ever make trails that go down? Why do they put lakes such a long way from roads? Why weren't people born with wings?

I was afraid the trail was never going to end.

Suddenly we came around a corner and there it was — Bear Lake. It was a beautiful spot of silver and blue right beneath the rock cliffs. Around it were wildflowers and boulders and trees with soft, green needles.

It was spectacular, but something was missing.

"Where are the bears?" I asked.

Mr. Sims raised his hand and pointed.

"Just one bear," he said. "Right there.

7
Bear Lake

Mr. Sims and Tim both helped me see the bear at Bear Lake.

"There's his head at that end," said Tim.

"See his nose?" pointed Mr. Sims.

"His back is under the cliff," said Tim.

"His front feet are pointing at us," said Mr. Sims.

I didn't want to believe what I was hearing.

"You mean it's called Bear Lake because it's *shaped* like a bear?" I asked.

"Sure," said Tim. "What did you think?"

I didn't answer. I slumped down on the grass. Tim looked at me funny.

"I'm going to go visit some friends," he said. He went off into the rocks.

"Find a place to perch, my tired Robyn," said Mr. Sims. "Eat a few worms. You'll soon feel better."

Mr. Sims went down to the lake to fish. I sat on a rock and felt sorry for myself. At last I opened my lunch.

It was a huge lunch. There were sandwiches, cheese, pickles, fruit, cookies and chocolate bars. I ate them all. Thank you Aunt Ellie!

Tim was sitting in the rocks eating his own lunch. I went to join him. He really had found some friends. They were a bit like gophers — except they had longer hair and they were way, way bigger. They were gophers the size of small dogs. They sat in the rocks just beyond Tim. Every once in a while one of them gave a long loud whistle.

"Marmots," said Tim. "They live up here."

While Tim ate, I took pictures. After that we watched Mr. Sims fish. Whenever he caught a fish, he let it go again. That's the way he likes to fish.

We saw an osprey do some fishing of its own. It kept what it caught.

It was a long way home. Aunt Ellie laughed when she saw me.

"You can be proud of yourself for walking all that way," she said. "And don't worry about picking up the garbage. I picked it up early because there was a bear down at the campground."

"A real bear?" I asked. "At the campground just down the road? And I wasn't here?"

I was trying to get excited about it, but I couldn't. I was too tired. Besides, Tim was looking at me funny again.

Getting excited would have to wait.

8
Campground disaster

The campground! Why hadn't I thought of it before? Bears like campgrounds. They like them on cartoons. They like them on movies. They even like them in real life!

That night, in our rooms way at the top of the lodge, I asked Tim if I could borrow his bike tomorrow to go down to the campground.

"It's something to do with bears, isn't it?" asked Tim.

"I just want to see one Tim," I said. "Everyone else in the world has seen them

— you, Anna, your mom and dad, Mr. Sims."

"OK, you can borrow a bike," said Tim. "But I'm coming too."

The next morning we set out. Tim had outgrown last year's bike and had a new one, so there was one for each of us. Squirrel came along too.

It was early. Most of the campground was still asleep. Squirrel and Tim and I stopped to watch the sun slide down the mountain peak. It was beautiful and I took a picture. The first rays of the sun turned the rock to gold.

That's when we heard it — a rustling in the bushes. My heart gave a thump but I closed my lips tight. I was *not* going to start yelling. My feet were not going to run away. Slowly, slowly we turned.

Just up the hill behind us, something was moving in the bushes. It was big enough to make the bushes sway and bend. And this time, from the way Squirrel's nose was moving, it wasn't a human.

Again the bushes moved. Squirrel began to quiver. Tim and I had the same thought at the same time. We'd better get hold of Squirrel. Fast.

Tim and I lunged for him. Squirrel was way ahead of us. With a great howl he took off up the hill toward the bushes.

At that moment the animal
pushed its way into the open.

"Porcupine!" shouted Tim.
"No!"

"Stop Squirrel!" I cried.
Too late.

9
Poor Squirrel

Poor Squirrel. Twelve quills in his nose and two of them were pretty deep.

"It's not the first porcupine he's run into," said Aunt Ellie. She helped Tim and I pull the quills out. "He should know by now."

But I could tell by the number of dog biscuits she gave him afterwards that she felt sorry for him.

Tim and I sat on the back steps after Aunt Ellie had gone.

"I was really, really scared back there," I said.

"You weren't the only one," said Tim.

"If it had been a bear, Squirrel could have gotten hurt a lot worse than just a few quills," I said.

Tim reached over and gave the dog a hug. Tim really loved Squirrel. So did I.

"And if it had been a bear, it might have taken after us too," I said.

"It might have," said Tim. "It's happened to people before."

That night I wrote a letter to Marie. I told her I'd given up looking for bears.

"Maybe I'm scared of them after all," I wrote to her. "Or maybe I'm just smarter since Squirrel's been hurt."

The crazy thing is, once I got started writing, I just kept going. Even without seeing a bear, I had lots to tell Marie. I told her about Anna chasing Uncle Paul out of the sheets. I told her about the hike to Bear Lake. Hey, maybe I was going to have some great summer stories after all! Grant the twerp might not think they were neat, but I did!

And when my photos came back, I'd have pictures to send the twins. They'd like pictures of marmots just as much as pictures of bears. I'd have other pictures too.

I was happy. Things were great. I was lucky to be having a great summer at Thunder

Mountain. I didn't need to see bears. Bears probably weren't anywhere near what they were cracked up to be. I was cured of bears once and for all.

But sometimes, just when you think you've got everything under control, the world decides to play a trick on you.

10
Bears!

"Robyn? Are you brave enough yet?"

"I'm brave enough," I said.

I knew Tim was talking about the roof. Tonight was the perfect night. It was hot and sticky in our bedrooms. On the roof it would be cool and dark and just right.

Tim boosted me up through the window. The shingles of the roof were rough against my knees and the palms of my hands. I helped him climb up after me.

We sat side by side and looked up at the night sky. The stars in the mountains must be brighter than anywhere else on earth. A zillion stars in a never-ending blackness — that's what we saw. There are so many of them they just sweep you away.

"There's the Big Dipper and the Little Dipper," I said.

"The Big Bear and the Little Bear," said Tim, "if you add a few more stars."

The Big Bear and the Little Bear. They'd been right above me all along.

And then I looked down. I don't know why, maybe we have senses we don't even

know about. I looked down and I saw them.

Bears. Three of them. Sliding out of the shadows of the trees.

"Tim," I whispered

They were huge. Their long hair was silver under the stars. Their bodies moved with power and ease. Wonderful power. Wonderful ease. Bears.

"Grizzlies," whispered Tim. "The first one's the mom, I think. The other two are cubs, almost full grown."

They stopped on the lawn beneath us. They lifted their noses to test the air. They paused. Motionless.

A wonder as great as the stars seemed to fill me. And I was scared too. I was perfectly safe, but I was scared. They were so big. So powerful.

Then they were moving again. The mother turned swiftly on her back legs. The cubs followed. With long, loping strides they melted into the darkness beyond the

cabins. They were gone as silently as they had come.

The stars shone. The air cooled.

Tim and I climbed back through the window. Quietly, so as not to lose the magic, we said goodnight.

I climbed back into bed. I wasn't cured after all. I wanted to see bears. I would always want to see bears.

Perhaps, if I fell asleep quickly, they would walk once more out of the woods and into my dreams.

Meet four other great kids in the New First Novels Series:

Duff's Monkey Business

by Budge Wilson/ Illustrated by Kim LaFave

Duff is known for his vivid imagination. So when Duff announces he has discovered a monkey in the family barn nobody believes him. Just when everyone has had enough of Duff's tall tales a circus comes to town minus its star monkey. Could Duff be telling the truth after all?

Jan on the Trail

by Monica Hughes/ Illustrated by Carlos Freire

When Jan and Sarah learn that Patch, their beloved dog friend, has been lost, they decide to become detectives and find him. Following the trail isn't easy but the girls are resourceful. They set off to follow the clues with the hope of reuniting Patch with his new owner.

Lilly Plays her Part
By Brenda Bellingham/
Illustrated by Elizabeth Owen

Lilly is happy because she has been chosen to be Gretel in the school musical, *Hansel and Gretel.* She is really looking forward to the play until it becomes obvious to everyone that her best friend Minna has been miscast as the evil witch. They need someone to play the witch who can sing, act and cackle — Lilly! Lilly is very disappointed. She really wanted to be Gretel, not the evil witch. Lilly struggles with her new role until she discovers that playing a witch can be fun.

Morgan's Secret
By Ted Staunton/ Illustrated by Bill Slavin

When Morgan's best friend Charlie tells him a secret he swears he can keep one. But then Morgan is assigned Aldeen Hummel, the Godzilla of Grade 3, as his science partner and the trouble begins. Aldeen makes everyone nervous. She makes Morgan so nervous the secret slips out. What will Morgan have to do to stop Aldeen from blabbing? Will Charlie ever forgive him?

Look for these New First Novels!

Meet Duff
Duff's Monkey Business
Duff the Giant Killer

Meet Jan
Jan on the Trail
Jan and Patch
Jan's Big Bang

Meet Lilly
Lilly's Good Deed
Lilly to the Rescue

Meet Robyn
Robyn Looks for Bears
Robyn's Want Ad
Shoot for the Moon, Robyn

Meet Morgan
Morgan's Secret
Morgan and the Money
Morgan Makes Magic

Meet Carrie
Carrie's Crowd
Go For It, Carrie

Meet Marilou
Marilou on Stage

Meet Max
Max the Superhero

Meet Mikey
Mikey Mite's Best Present
Good For You, Mikey Mite!
Mikey Mite Goes to School
Mikey Mite's Big Problem

Meet Mooch
Missing Mooch
Mooch Forever
Hang On, Mooch!
Mooch Gets Jealous
Mooch and Me

Meet Raphael
Video Rivals

Meet the Swank Twins
The Swank Prank
Swank Talk

Meet Will
Will and His World

Formac Publishing Company Limited
5502 Atlantic Street, Halifax, Nova Scotia B3H 1G4
Orders: 1-800-565-1975 Fax: (902) 425-0166